9404158

EJ

Gould, Deborah.

Aaron's shirt /

Aaron's Shirt

by Deborah Gould
illustrations by Cheryl Harness

BRADBURY PRESS
New York

Bradbury Press
An Affiliate of Macmillan, Inc.
866 Third Avenue, New York, NY 10022
Collier Macmillan Canada, Inc.
Printed and bound in the United States of America
First American Edition
10 9 8 7 6 5 4 3 2

The text of this book is set in 16 point Souvenir Gothic Light.
The illustrations are rendered in watercolor.

LIBRARY OF CONGRESS CATALOGING-IN-PUBLICATION DATA
Gould, Deborah.
Aaron's shirt/by Deborah Gould; illustrated by Cheryl Harness.   p.
Summary: Aaron loves his favorite shirt and, after wearing it
constantly for two years, is reluctant to admit that he has outgrown it.
ISBN 0-02-736351-1
[1. Clothing and dress—Fiction.]   I. Harness, Cheryl. ill.   II. Title.
PZ7.G723Aar   1989 [E]—dc19   88-10414 CIP AC

For Marjory, who listened
from the beginning
— D. G.

To Ray and Elaine
— C. H.

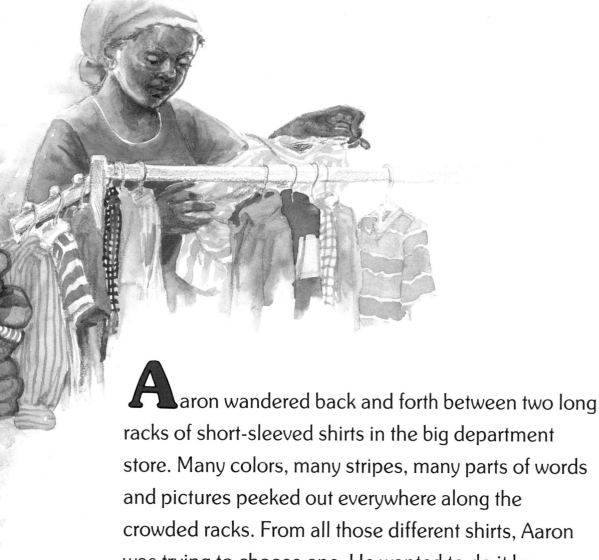

Aaron wandered back and forth between two long racks of short-sleeved shirts in the big department store. Many colors, many stripes, many parts of words and pictures peeked out everywhere along the crowded racks. From all those different shirts, Aaron was trying to choose one. He wanted to do it by himself, but his mother was making him hurry now. She held out two shirts with dinosaurs on the front and said, "Look, Aaron, these are nice. Do you want the green one or the blue?"

Aaron was getting tired of shopping. He was
about to choose the green shirt when another caught
his eye. Its bold red and white stripes seemed to shine
right at him. He reached out eagerly and touched it.
Then, holding the bright striped shirt in both hands, he
said clearly, "This is the one I want."

Mom quickly checked the shirt and the label.
"This should give you room to grow," she said. "Let's
buy it now and hope it fits. We've really got to go." They
headed for the cash register, and soon Aaron was
carrying the shirt in a crinkly store bag.

When they got home, Aaron changed right into the new shirt. He stood very straight, feeling the crisp clean cloth on his shoulders, back, and chest. Mom looked pleased, but his big sister, Lydia, said, "That shirt is kind of baggy." Aaron didn't care what she said, he liked the shirt so much. He ran outside to wear it in the warm spring afternoon.

The next day he wore the shirt, and he won a huge
stuffed bear in the Spring Fair raffle.

When he wore it the day after, he made a new friend, Tim. There was something special about that shirt!

Aaron wanted to sleep in it, but his mom said, "Absolutely not."

The next morning he wanted to wear it again,
but he couldn't find it. "Where's my shirt?" he cried.

"Your new shirt is in the clothes hamper," said
Mom, "but you have lots of other clean ones."

"I don't want to wear any other shirt," Aaron said.

"Well, you'll have to, until I wash that one," his
mother insisted.

Aaron wore other shirts only while his favorite went through the wash. Sometimes he waited by the dryer while the shirt was tumbling inside. As soon as the dryer stopped, he would open the door, find his warm fragrant shirt, and change into it.

He wore the shirt throughout the spring and summer. He wore it in restaurants and on the beach. He wore it climbing mountains and visiting the zoo. He wore it wherever and whenever he could until the cold weather began.

"You've worn this shirt seventy-nine times at least," said Mom, folding it neatly for winter storage.

"Do you have to put it away for the whole winter?" Aaron asked.

"Yes, it will last longer if we let it hibernate. You can wear it again in the spring," she reassured him.

The winter was cold and long, but on the first spring day Aaron found the storage box and took out his favorite shirt. It wasn't as big or as bright as he remembered, but he was glad to be inside it again.

He wore it to school that morning and many days
after that.

One afternoon playing hide-and-seek, Aaron felt the shirt catch and rip on a broken wire fence. Aaron ran home. Luckily his mom was back from work. He begged her to mend the torn place right away.

"Calm down, Aaron, please," said Mom. "Just put on another shirt. I'll sew this after supper."

Aaron could hardly wait for supper to end. He didn't even want his ice cream. Lydia teased, "You think your shirt is more important than dessert."

Finally Mom got down the sewing box. When she sat on the couch to mend the ragged seam, Aaron sat beside her and watched. "You can do some too," she said, guiding his hand to push and pull the needle through the cloth.

Aaron was glad he helped with the sewing. He liked to touch the line of stitches whenever he put the shirt on. But he didn't wear it as much as before; he wanted to keep it safe.

When the cold weather came this time, Aaron
gave the shirt to his mother to pack away. She
hesitated with the shirt in her hand. "This really should
go in the giveaway box, not the storage box. You'll be
too big for it by spring."

"No, I won't," Aaron protested.

"You can't promise not to grow," Mom said, but
she packed the shirt in the storage box.

On the morning of the first warm day in March, Aaron unpacked the shirt himself and tried it on. The sleeves were tight under his arms, and the whole shirt felt small, but he didn't want to take it off.

At breakfast Lydia said, "You know, your belly button shows." Aaron pulled the shirt down hard in front. He felt it pull up high in back.

Mom said, "Aaron, you have got to admit it doesn't fit. It should be in the giveaway box right now."

Lydia argued, "Really, it's so worn out, no other kid will take it. It should go in the rag bag."

"Lydia, hush!" Mom scolded as Aaron rushed out of the kitchen.

In his room with the door shut, Aaron searched for a place to hide his shirt. He wouldn't let it be given away or used as a rag, ever. He didn't want to hide it, but what else could he do?

All at once he knew. There, slumped in a corner of his room, was his big old stuffed bear. As soon as Aaron squeezed the shirt over the bear's thick head, the rest was easy. Smoothing the shirt down around the firm furry body, Aaron realized how perfectly it fit.

Later when Mom saw the bear, she said, "Now, there is someone who can wear your shirt all year, even in winter."

Then Lydia added, "He'll never outgrow it either." And that was exactly what Aaron wanted to hear.